W9-BMR-436

Winter Friends

By Gabrielle Reyes
Illustrated by The Artifact Group

SCHOLASTIC INC.

ISBN 978-0-545-59210-9
© 2013 MEG. All Rights Reserved.

PUPPY IN MY POCKET® and all related titles, logos and characters are trademarks of MEG.
Licensed by Licensing Works!®

Published by Scholastic Inc. SCHOLASTIC and associated logos are trademarks and/or registered trademarks of Scholastic Inc.

12 11 10 9 8 7 6 5 4 3 2 1   13 14 15 16 17 18/0
Printed in the U.S.A.   40

Designed by Angela Jun
First printing, November 2013

Buddy woke up wagging his tail. He had been sick for a week, but was finally feeling better! He hopped off his bed to go tell his friends.

"Hey, Montana! Guess what?" Buddy barked. "Yesterday, the doctor said I have to stay home today and rest." He sniffled a little. "But tomorrow, I can go back to school!"

"That's great!" Montana replied. "But you aren't the only one not going to school today. Look outside!"

Buddy glanced out the window and his eyes opened wide. "It snowed!"

"Sure did, Buddy," said Spike. "School is canceled. It's a snow day!"

The puppies couldn't wait to get outside.

"Fuji, let's go sledding on the Big Hill!" Montana exclaimed.

"That's a great idea," Fuji replied. "I can't wait to go really fast!"

"Ivy and I are going to make snowdogs," said Spike.
"I better find my mittens!" Ivy said, running to her room.
Everyone was excited to play in the snow. Everyone
except Buddy.

Buddy couldn't help but feel jealous watching Fuji and Montana take the sled out.

"Don't forget about the jump in the middle of the hill," Buddy told them. "If you hit it just right, you'll—*cough, cough*—go flying."

"Thanks, Buddy!" said Fuji. "We wish you could come with us. Get some rest today, okay?"

Buddy nodded as they went out the door. *I want to go sledding, too,* he thought.

Buddy padded into the living room, feeling miserable. He grabbed a tissue and blew his nose. As he passed the window, he saw Spike and Ivy playing in the backyard. They were making a shaggy snowdog.

"That looks like fun," said Buddy with a sigh. "The snow is perfect for building snowdogs—and having a snowball fight, too."

9

Buddy's throat still felt a little sore, so he went to the kitchen to get something to drink.

"Hey, Buddy," Freddy barked as he walked through the door. "How are you feeling?"

"Oh!" Buddy jumped. "Hi, Freddy. I didn't think anyone was still home."

"I was in my room working on this! Check it out."
Buddy looked at the piece of paper Freddy put down
on the table. "I'm going to make the best snow fort ever."
Freddy trotted out of the kitchen to get his snow gear.

Buddy was amazed. He wished he could help Freddy make the fort. A few minutes later, Freddy came back wearing his coat and hat, and saw Buddy's sad face. "Aw, Buddy . . . don't worry. You'll be all better soon."

SNOW FORT

MOVIE ROOM

SNACK ROOM

"But all the snow will be melted soon!" Buddy yelped.

Freddy looked thoughtful. "Why don't we watch a movie when I get back?" he suggested.

"Yeah, okay. . . ." said Buddy, looking down at the ground. "Have fun. . . ." and he walked down the hall to his room with his tail between his legs.

Freddy watched him go. "Poor pup," he said. He
grabbed his drawing and headed out the door. But as
soon as he saw all the snow, he had a thought. "There's
got to be a way to play in the snow inside. . . ."

Later that afternoon, Buddy woke up from a nap and jumped out of bed. He was about to rush out the door to see his friends when he remembered everyone was playing in the snow. He sat back down and sighed.

Suddenly, something made his ears perk up. He heard noises coming from the living room. "I wonder who's home," Buddy said to himself.

17

Buddy ran down the hall to see Spike and Ivy
huddled over a box on the table.

"Hi, Buddy!" Ivy said. "Freddy told us you were
feeling left out of the snow day, so—"

"So we looked online and found a way to bring the snow to you!" Spike jumped in. "Check it out!"

Buddy put his paws in the box of white stuff in front of Spike and Ivy. He couldn't believe it. Spike and Ivy had made snow!

"We made it using some cornstarch," Ivy said proudly. "We can even build little snowdogs with this."

"Awesome!" Buddy said. "I want to make a snow-beagle!"

A little while later, Fuji and Montana came in from the kitchen. "Look, Buddy! We made snow ice cream!" said Montana.

"Here, try it!" invited Fuji.

Buddy took a lick. "*Mmm* . . . This tastes like . . . vanilla!" he said. "Freddy will love it!" Buddy paused to look around. "Is Freddy back, too?"

"I'm right here, Buddy," a voice called. Buddy looked
over and saw a pile of pillows and blankets coming his way.
It was Freddy! "Since you can't go outside to build a snow
fort, we're going to build a snow fort inside!"

"Wow!" Buddy cried.

Buddy and the puppies spent the rest of the
afternoon working on the snow fort. They created
separate rooms by draping blankets over couch cushions.

"Hey, Freddy—check this out!" Buddy hollered, showing him the tunnel he had finished off with a snowy-white blanket.

"Fantastic!" said Freddy.

Later that evening, Buddy sat in front of the fort
enjoying another scoop of homemade snow ice cream.

"Thanks to you pups, I had the best snow day ever!"
he told his friends.

The next morning, Buddy was the very first pup outside!